HARMONY

BY WENDY J. MARAIS

Balboa Press books may be ordered through booksellers or by contacting:

Balboa Press
A Division of Hay House
1663 Liberty Drive
Bloomington, IN 47403
www.balboapress.com
1 (877) 407-4847

Because of the dynamic nature of the Internet, any web addresses or links contained in this book may have changed since publication and may no longer be valid. The views expressed in this work are solely those of the author and do not necessarily reflect the views of the publisher, and the publisher hereby disclaims any responsibility for them.

Any people depicted in stock imagery provided by Getty Images are models, and such images are being used for illustrative purposes only.
Certain stock imagery © Getty Images.

Library of Congress Control Number: 2018908929

ISBN: 978-1-9822-0871-4 (sc)
ISBN: 978-1-9822-0872-1 (e)

Print information available on the last page.

Balboa Press rev. date: 10/25/2018

BALBOA.
PRESS
A DIVISION OF HAY HOUSE

Dedicated to Samantha with love

To my Mom, for all she is and all she once was. I love you, Mom.

Special thanks to Candy and Shannon for taking such good care of me at the library while
I wrote the initial part of this book during our memorable summer together.

Rose R. for all your love and support.

To the real Princess Maxine and Prince Michael for the special people they once were in my life.

To Michael Richard Miller for his loving support and encouragement!

To Marsha Manion at Balboa Press for her help and faith in me.

To Salvatore Lupusella without whose presence in my life, this book would have
never been written. For giving me the greatest gift of all Samantha.

For Theresa Arone for being the Zia of all Zia's thank you for your presence in my life and Samantha's.

To Jay Borelli, may god bless you and your family always.

Laurie Elia for her outstanding and dedicated friendship.

To Frankie R., a very good friend.

To Glenn Marais for being a prince amongst brothers. (a kiss for Andre too)

May God bless you all and hold you in the palm of his hand.

VEE
XTENSIONS
Hair & Lashes

Table of Contents

The Introduction

If this is your first time reading Harmony and you are reading it by yourself, then follow the instructions and make it a more enjoyable read. I find myself to be laughing and enjoying the story more by doing this. It's ok to laugh out loud when you're by yourself. It's ok to cry because it takes a stronger person to cry than to hold it in and a stronger person still to realize what it is behind those tears.

If you are reading Harmony for the first time as part of a group – then your group leader will explain all the fun, exciting and challenging parts of Harmony with you as you go.

Harmony the Song

I was walking down the street
Looking for a new life beat
When suddenly it came to me from the sky
It has been there all along in the winds that refuse to die

Chorus

My harmony can you give your love to me – my
Harmony, my sweet, sweet harmony
Do you feel the laugher in my smile?
The laughter that comes from deep inside, my harmony
Harmony will you teach me more than how to fly
Will you help me to bring the love back to my tired eyes?

Occasionally I think of the girl I once was
And look at the girl I have become
Looking for the woman that I dream of becoming
When you reach into your heart
Does it tear you apart?
Or make you begin that wonderful new start

The one that starts in your heart

My harmony can you give your love to me-
My harmony, my sweet, sweet harmony
Do feel the laughter in my smile?
The laughter that comes from deep inside, my harmony
Harmony will you teach more than how to fly
Will you help me to bring the love back into my tired eyes?

Occasionally I think of the girl I once was
And I look at the girl I have become
Looking for that woman I dream of becoming
When you reach into your heart
Does it tear you a part?
Or make you begin that wonderful new start
The one that starts in your heart

Chorus

My harmony can you give your love to me –
My harmony, my sweet, sweet harmony
Do you feel the laughter in my smile?
The laughter that comes from deep inside, my harmony
Harmony will you teach more than how to fly
Will help me to bring get the love back in my eyes?

Harmony won't you give your love to me
Can you teach me to love?
Can you show the me the way to find love?
I look into your eyes and a part of my heart sighs
While another part slowly dies
Harmony can you give your love to me
To show me how to reach my heart
To have the life that belongs to me.
Harmony sing slowly to my heart
Let us be together never far apart

Chorus

My harmony, can you give your love to me
My harmony, my sweet, sweet harmony
Do you feel the laughter in my smile?
The laughter that comes from deep inside, my harmony
Will you teach me more than how to fly?
Will you bring the love back into my eyes?
Harmony, my sweet sweet harmony………………fade out

My name is Harmony, once upon a time I lived in a place filled with darkness.

My own darkness, the darkness that is brought about by the lack of hope, the darkness filled with a lack of feeling loved. Perhaps my own expectations are too high, or not high enough. Let us decide through our journey together. The darkness of that lack of love caused me to reach out to others who showed any interest in me so tightly that I drove them crazy with my adoration. In my eagerness to please, I lost myself in their lives' so that they would accept me. Not realizing that they accepted the real me when they met me and expressed interest in the first place. Am I going too fast? I tend to do that sometimes, to my regret. Let me know if I am, please?

Then what happens is they (the new friends or old friends) start to feel so overly gripped by my ever-growing attention that they push me away, sometimes quite harshly and that sinks me into a deeper hole of darkness. This is my story of how I came out of the darkness and into the light, as well as the many steps I took on my adventure of a lifetime!

Understanding that love, true love is the key to everything is the beginning of any other journey. Without love of something or someone there is nothing.

Love is about freedom, the freedom to enjoy a person and respect enough for them; not only to let them go but to help them build their own dreams. It is not allowing yourself to become part of their hopes and dreams unless you truly want to be. True acceptance of their hopes and dreams for themselves even if they don't fit into your picture of what you imagined. Unless you have decided to build a life together and that will never happen without freedom, loyalty and respect. More importantly it is about not losing yourself within their hopes and dreams. It is about having the strength to know when to support someone and when to say no!

Life, Love and Career

*What we should do now is write down our true hopes and dreams for ourselves. In our three major categories: love, life and career. Does that sound good? We will come back to it afterwards. Take time out right now to do this together, as a group or singularly whichever you feel more comfortable with.

Love

Career

Life

YOURSELF

TWO MOST IMPORTANT PEOPLE

Then when you are finished writing your own dreams. You can look at the two people you care the most about in your life. Whether it be your best friend, your brother or sister, your mom or dad and ask yourself if you know what their hopes and dreams are? If you don't, go find out! Now! Well maybe not this second; if you are at school or doing important work. Well you get my general meaning. If these are the most important people in your life you should know there hopes and dreams, if you don't you should find out!

Name of a first person

_____

Know what the hopes and dreams you want for them? Why and why not?

_____

_____

_____

_____

Name of a second person

_____

Know what the hopes and dreams you want for them? Why and why not?

_____

_____

_____

_____

Remember that no matter what you want for them, ultimately, it's about what they want themselves - nothing less. When you gain the self-esteem and self-respect to let go, then and only then are you set free. Only then can you feel that you are worthy of all the love they have to offer you since the beginning.

So, this is how my journey begins. This is the first of many, let's call them brain jolters! Did that entice a series of lightning flashes to go through your head? Raise your left foot if it did!

School was a place to congregate until next weekend's party, and to decide if we were going to sneak out of the house to get there. My parents were ultraconservative to the point that I would change clothes and put my makeup on in the bathroom at school. So, they taught me to lie rather than respect my judgement; just an honest observation.

Half the parties I snuck out to were just to see if I could be away with it. And I got it in a lot more trouble at the ones they said I could go to, kind of ironic isn't it?

I was in science class thinking hard about a word I should know the meaning of but for the life of me couldn't remember. I was so frustrated it was laughable, so off I went to the lady's room, good escape for now.

The ladies room, why they call it that I don't know, do you? Personally, I call it gossip center, the bully room and the nasty room. There is where the nastiest of the nastiest conservations go on. That's where I was sitting on the toilet one afternoon and heard three girls talking about their friend how was so nasty and so mean to everyone. I was totally appalled when leaning towards the door to listen more carefully and closely when they said,

"Yes, and how are we going to help Harmony, we have to tell her?"

I almost fell off my seat. My heart thumped, and I was completely humiliated. And thought I was so nice to everyone. I put my hands over my ears and waited until they left. I then crawled out the door. When I looked down and an amazing thing had happened I had turned into a caterpillar, all purple, green and lilac. I slowly made my way out the door and that was the beginning of my adventure.

The Old Man and His Loving Words!

Now let me tell you something, things are much different down here, everything is taller! I went to sleep under a tree. I think it was a few hours later when I woke up and discovered that my life was beginning over.

I found myself in the middle of a black sandy beach with big waves smashing the most beautiful charcoal grey cliff. As the waves rolled in they created a loud boom and as they rolled back out it was an almost silent and peaceful feeling. You could smell the salt of ocean. It was so nice, I could have laid there forever but of course that is not part of the story. I must make it through the journey or you won't be able to help someone else with their journey.

Well I slowly turned my head sideways and amazingly enough there was this old man with a face that looked like it was carved by god himself. His cheek bones were high, the lines on his face deep and skin was a mahogany brown, he smelt like a mixture of cinnamon, cloves, ginger and oranges. You know like those oranges that some mom's make at Christmas time with the cloves in them. Close your eyes, now take a deep breath in, can you smell them the oranges? His eyes, his eyes they were the most beautiful green eyes I have ever seen, they were the color of emeralds, dazzling, extremely mesmerizing green.

He gently touched my face, and said to me "it is ok, my girl, the world will turn out alright for you." I looked at him and I said, "Tell me how?"

Then he smiled with the most beautiful white teeth and whispered, "If I told you the answer it would mean nothing to you and you would learn nothing. First you must close your eyes and think of a world of your own, no one else's but one that is for you and only you. Then you should draw a map in your mind that includes you and your partners as well as friends.

Then write down qualities in life that are important to you. Then, when you meet new people you must not deviate from these qualities you desire in them. Or your path will become misdirected and it may take you a very long time to come back to where you belong, if ever. Remember to look after your own interests and develop them with care, with the guidance of people who have similar goals and beliefs.

When you begin your search for your other half ask what kind of person you would not only like to begin your life with but what kind of person you would your life to end your life with. Should they make you laugh or cry, should they be your true partner in everyway, do you need someone to lean on sometimes? Or to stand beside you? Are they capable of giving you that? Are you capable of giving that in return? Make sure they never lie to you and you never lie to them. Always be loyal and faithful, never be disrespectful to them, especially since it takes such a long time of looking to find the right people.

All the while I looked at him and found his eyes to be so mesmerizing that I knew I would never be able to forget the words he told me.

I looked at him and I said, "I am lost, and I will find my way, thank you for your kind words. You are right, I will be careful about who I let into my life. Let's go through the qualities of the people that you would like to have in your life. Are they sports minded, do they like to read, be open to writing a little bit or a lot? Think about it very carefully, these types of decisions can be tough to make but, in the end, will be very rewarding.

Now look around you at your friends. Are they there for the right reasons in life? Are their qualities, good or bad? Now can you accept the bad ones? Do you show enough appreciation for the good ones?

Let's talk a bit about these qualities or traits that we should look for in others, and hopefully find in ourselves, say them out loud and write them down as fast as you can.

Qualities or Traits you would like in a friend.

_____

_____

_____

_____

When you are done this, go through the list and give your personal definition of what the words mean.

_____

_____

_____

_____

Harmony

Ok back to the story of Harmony.

armony closes her eyes for just a moment and when she wakes up she is only half caterpillar and she is walking now. Does this mean that she has made some sort of progression, towards the right way of thinking? Although for the life of her she can't figure out why her legs are still green?

She is in a big city with lots of turns and city noises and lights, she thinks its her city yet somehow different, imagine yourself in this position with these thoughts and feelings running through your head. So, she decided to set out and find her home and maybe her mom or dad who can tell her what this is all about? After all they are always telling her that if she listens to them it will save her a lot of trouble in the long run, oh wow, maybe they were right.

She begins to walk and walk, asking many people for directions and they all misdirect her, telling her the wrong way to go. Like they want her to stay lost and never find her way home. She becomes disoriented and scared while running helter smelter looking for her home.

Where she will be safe? She comes to realize that where she is in the future, some of the streets are changed; the houses that once looked new are now old.

Finally, she recognized the house of the old lady down the street who always made her some crazy knitted thing for Christmas. But she never said thank you, she was going to say thank you the next time she saw her. She says out loud "but what if I never see her again?"

Suddenly there was this beautiful little pixie girl, with a dark complexion and hair that is white blonde, and her blue eyes were bigger than jawbreakers. I love jawbreakers! Well I did when I was a kid, how about you? Or those little black candies that turned into pink in the middle, anyway off topic. Suddenly, the little girl let's call her Candice, she took my hand. She never said a word yet somehow, I knew she was guiding me the right way. We walked in a companionable silence and then she stopped and turned me round and round, faster and faster, and when I stopped I was in front of my old house.

Happy Birthday

I ran up to the front door and knocked and knocked. No answer! Figures, usually someone is always home. I went around the back and looked in the kitchen window. There was a lady sitting at the table by herself with a little birthday cake in front!

Then suddenly she turned and looked at me right in the eyes and it was me, about 30 years older. She said out loud, "See this is what will happen to you if you don't heed the lessons you are learning on this journey, the second chance that you have been given. A second chance, or probably more like a tenth or eleventh! Go and follow that road and be happy. So, you don't turn out like me alone on your birthday with no one around you to love you and to cherish you. Take time to find those right people and now get out of here your ruining my birthday. Get!

I am so tired this is just unbelievable, my own version Scrooge, but worse, I am all green, and at least we know that happened to Scrooge.

The Red Book and Blessings

She shakes her head and walks away very discouraged. She felt so light and happy after leaving the old man then she realizes she never did the exercise, she pulls out her red book and she starts to write under a tree and to write. After a short while she falls asleep dreaming of the pixie-girl Candice.

In my dream she keeps telling me over and over and over "do what you are going to do, and all will be right. Do it with kindness and without expectations of any kind in return, that way you will always be blessed." The words rolled in my mind all night. When I wake up that thought became my mantra, I would try my best to live up to that expectation of myself, and to apply what the old man had told me about who I should make a part of my life and who I should not.

My day started with a spring in my step and oh my I have my arms back completely, which I should have realized when I was writing today. I got so caught up in the words I didn't notice my arms. This is incredible, it must be that when I learn something new I receive a part of myself back. Something beautiful, something I always took for granted my legs and now my arms. I feel blessed, I am blessed!

The Long Walk to Consciousness!

As I walked down the long road on that day and for many days afterwards I was alone with thoughts which gave me time to reflect on the things I had begun to learn.

I thought of different scenarios in which I would tell my friends, so they would be impressed! Then I realized that was who I was before and that was a part of what I needed to get rid of. The need to impress, to realize that was something already had inside of me.

I walked, and I thought of the qualities of what I would like from my life partner; laughter, dancing lots of dancing even in the kitchen, lots of affection and someone who would help me grow but also protect me from harm; always. Someone who was honest, loyal and someone who would want to spend their time with me as much as I would spend my time with them. A reader, a writer, and maybe a piano player, I have always wanted to play the piano. Someone who liked to travel to exotic places and who would be adventurous with me. I thought of the work I would like to do. Was I smart enough or for that matter, dedicated enough or even talented? That is when I realized that by questioning those things I would never achieve anything. I need to believe that I was all those things! Just by dreaming about it made me good enough. Therefore, now I needed to gather the right skills and to never stop learning those skills so that I could do anything I wanted to do. I could do anything I could dream I could do..

The Man and the Linden Tree

One day when I was longing for home and some one to talk to, I came across a man, he was sitting on the ground under a beautiful tree that smelled of lemons, as the wind blew through the leaves I could smell nothing but lemons. I think it is called a Linden tree. Close your eyes and imagine that spell that smell let it run through you slowly and then feel it in your pores. Can you feel it? The sweet smell of lemons. It is a nice feeling, isn't it?

This man, he had the most incredible gentle eyes with the longest eyelashes. He asked me my name and I told him, he sat with his body in the most upright position with his head cocked to the side and started to smile very slowly. He was intriguing very intriguing. "Do you think you could help me find my way home?" I asked him.

"You are already home; therefore, you took and that is why you are with me now. I have been waiting for you for a very long time, you must walk very slowly, or dilly dally a lot?

Now this guy was starting to freak me out, there is no way that this could be real. Really, I slapped the side of my head, this whole thing was like something out of Alice in Wonderland and I was starting to feel like I was going further down the hole instead of back up.

"Ok if you have been waiting for me and I am already home, what are we going to do next."

"I am going to show you how to live your life and teach you a new way to go."

Now something about the way, he said that made the hair stand up on my arms, which are still green by the way but getting lighter every day, more natural looking, oh that's funny, I must laugh! Give me a minute to collect myself.

Ok I well I don't have anything else pressing in my agenda right now. So why not just go with the flow and see what happens? Yet somewhere in the back of my head I heard the old man's voice telling me to be careful of who I let into my life and to be careful how you affect other people's lives. There is something about his voice that makes my head listen very carefully. With a feeling of unfathomable hope, I followed him.

I had over the months of walking and finding my way here been blessed so many times by what I call the kindness of strangers, people who held my hand to keep me out of the way of a passing car, or people who fed me when I was hungry. People who held my bags or carried them for me when I was too cold or hungry to allow them not to, people who stood beside me in little ways, and big ways. The kindness of strangers, the young man in the purple shirt who smiled so brightly and carried my heavy bags inside for me. The wise old man and on and on the list goes.

I was really missing my friends from home, clap your hands if you have a friend you would miss if you turned into a caterpillar like me and was wandering around for months. My mom and dad must be worried, going to get grounded for this one.

Ok back to the story, the man and I worked together, ate together for many months. He was very private and sometimes would get very angry if I asked the wrong questions or said the wrong things. He made me want to go crazy. I made him crazy, but every day I learnt a new lesson from him, about honesty, humility, hope and in some way's, I grew to almost love him.

While I worked he spoke to me about the things that interested him, the history of Ferrari and the jewels of Monsieur Cartier. Did you know that Enzo Ferrari built a car right before he died called the F40? That car was total accumulation of his life's work. Enzo rode a British motorcycle called a Rudge. In 2006, Ferrari sold 5671 cars-635 in the UK, 1 V12 engineered car is sold for every v 8's. The most powerful racing car ever is the 660 bhp Enzi. Did you also know that Tessa Rosa – means red head in Italian? Enzo Ferrari wore sunglasses everywhere he went. Remind you of anyone? Did you know that racing cars were named for their project numbers? 640 and 641F1 cars were named that in the 80's? The first automatic Ferrari was built in 1976, the 400 GT. I could go on and on. But hey it is all cool. I love cars, how about you?

Now diamonds and big gems that is even cooler. But first let me explain about the work that we did, you see it was very interesting too! This man he had a stillness about him except for when he worked, then he moved with an agility and grace that was lovely to watch. He had a bike shop, his love of Enzo took him to bicycles and e-bikes, new bikes and old bikes. He fixed them and sold them.

We would work for hours listening to music everything from classical piano (great for concentration by the way) to the Bee Gee's and Aerosmith. Now for me the original Mrs. Bieber it was enlightening to say the least and not once have I listened to Justin since I got here, no offense Justin but I don't miss him, so much new stuff to assimilate.

At night we would eat and talk, which is how I started to learn all the things about the Ferrari's, Ebikes and Cartier.

The Game

Then one night I fell asleep and I had a dream, an amazing dream! In my dream my friend and I built a game. An amazing dream with ebikes, good guys, bad guys and a worldwide subway system. A logistics nightmare, but hey it's a dream and a game. Now listen up carefully because if you write a story or create a storyboard for the game and win the Harmony game challenge, you win a scholarship to towards the tuition of the school of your choice. Or an opportunity to build the game. The characters are here and the main story line – you develop and pick the challenges. You control the game. Email the completed story for your opportunity to win a scholarship and credit in the full version of this book. There will be three books in the trilogy. Your game will be added to that. Email to jazzled777@gmail.com with the title Harmony in the subject line. The winner will be announced at www.jazzled.world during December 2018.

Ok first in the game the world is threatened by air pollution, water pollution, the ice caps are melting releasing old viruses into the atmosphere and global warning has accelerated to a very high level. People must buy licenses to obtain clean air and water.

There is a legend that a blue diamond which is housed in the Smithsonian when held together with a blue diamond that is owned by Princess Maxine of Ireland will create a vortex which will cleanse the earth of its unnatural pollutants forever. A vortex would be created, the swirling blue diamond dust would attract all the pollutants and they would be swept into outer space. The diamond was stolen from the Smithsonian and this is when Princess Maxine's family came forward with the legend that could save the earth.

The story is that her grandma was the sister of Jeanne Toussaint and that Monsieur Cartier himself designed the setting of the flawless Blue Diamond. During the Second World War, her grandma escaped to America with the help of the French Resistance. She ran with a group of very talented and highly respected people, among them was a diamond cutter she called Sam.

Sam was a very talented, woman diamond cutter with an international reputation, which was very rare, as woman were seldom allowed into the inner circle of the Amsterdam diamond cutters. But then Sam's father didn't hesitate to train Sam in the art of diamond cutting the minute that he realized that Sam had a natural gifted eye for it.

Maxime's grandmother had the diamond sewed into the bodice of her dress, when she realized she was blessed with a huge opportunity. She decided to have the diamond cut in half, the stone was too recognizable unless it was cut.

Sam held the diamond in her hand looking at it in the light, studying the different angles picking the best spot to place the first cut. She slowly put the diamond on the table, picked up the cutter and hammer. With a swift movement she tapped the diamond, in that moment the room filled with the shining blue diamond that swirled around and round. The women were caught up in the dust `as they flew around the room slowly with a ballet type of grace. As the dust began to gently dissipate they gracefully landed on their feet. First, they looked up at each other to make sure they were fine but as they did, they glanced down on the table where unbelievably the diamond was now perfectly in two, not another cut would be needed. No polishing, no cleaning, no bruting (the art of insuring clarity and best angles.) none of the usual steps in the diamond cutting trade, the two identical blue stones were perfect! The room became still like a twinkly starry night, a deep voice filled the air, it said, "one day these two stones will become one with a power that will save the world", and then all was quiet and still again.

Folklore says that the diamond will clean the earth of all its pollutants. Because the stone was halved its power doubled instead of weakening. By bringing the two stones together again the power will be increased to immeasurable amounts. This power will cover the world which will create a vacuum type of a vortex that will take the pollutants out of the water and air then scatter it.

Draw two women doing ballet swirling with the blue diamond dust around them.

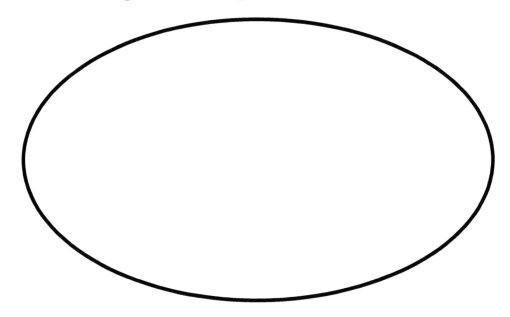

This how the legend started, and it continued to grow until Maxine's family decided that it was too dangerous to tell the story, so they stopped talking of the legend. One stone stayed with Maxine's grandmother and today Maxine wears it around her neck, never taking it off. Monsieur Cartier was pursued to design a unique and beautiful setting for stone. The stone was sold to a mysterious lady and was later donated to the Smithsonian, where it stayed. Until it was stolen, it was believed that the reason for this is to keep the world in turmoil and allow, as well allow evil people to take control of the clean air and water.

The first avatar is a blonde with big purple eyes. She is deaf, and she teaches the others to communicate through sign language. Her level of communication is so high that she sends her thoughts to her people without speaking.

Her name is Maxine, she moves with an amazing athletic grace. While wearing very artsy clothes and the large blue diamond on a white gold chain around her neck, her contributions to the team are invaluable. Her motivation is pure and completely innocent. Her charm is in her naiveté and her extreme intelligence. Maxine adds to the group because of her innocent approach to life. Her greatest gift and her biggest downfall.

Maxine is an Irish princess and she grew up in a beautiful castle in Tipperary. With many beautiful turrets and vines that grew up the castle walls.

Maxine came to America to join forces with the good guys and save the world from evil. She brought with her, her best friend and closest ally her twin brother, Prince Michael.

Prince Michael is tall with a cocky stance as if to say look at me world here I am. His heart is pure, he has no hidden challenges or emotions to overcome. He moves with unmatched agility and grace. His eyes are hazel, soft and yet piercing. He has a devilish wit and a keen brilliant mind. He is Maxine's protector—where she is naïve, he is worldly. He keeps her from harm at all costs. He drives a Harley Davidson e-bike and leads the army that Maxine commands. He is a natural born leader. He dresses in the top of the line designer clothes and he wears them well. His body is athletic and lanky with a regally daunting posture.

On his right hand he wears a pure white diamond almost the size of a robin's egg. The story of which will be the center of another Harmony series. It is an oval stone, set in white gold by Monsieur Cartier. Just one of a kind setting there is not another one of its kind.

It is through his leadership that all the riders learn to ride their ebikes, their scooters and other electric vehicles that are part of Maxine's army of good guys. Although Prince Michael is the only one who rides a Harley. Prince Michael has an assistant whose name is Jonathan, he is learning all about ebikes and all the things that Prince Michael can teach him. He likes to play games and has a good sense of humor and a good heart. The evil side tries many times to convert him over to the bad side. He is a short, dark haired young man with a very handsome face. He likes to wear team shirts. Plays a mean game of Tiger Ball, which is a game we start to play in the next adventure of Harmony.

The third is a dark-haired male, extremely well educated, the top of his class. Likes to play chess and he is extremely talented with numbers. He holds the key to the code that unlocks the box that holds the gem; that could save the world. He is unaware of this though and the box can only be unlocked when he develops a conscious and realizes that good will overcome evil every time.

As he grows a bigger conscious and a deeper respect of life he becomes more and more loved by the group. Show us how he gets to that point. Do you see the challenges that he faces and how he deals with them? He has long black hair and a wicked yet endearing, childlike smile with white teeth that are slightly crooked yet very attractive. You can name him anything you want.

He has an evil twin. Someone who is evil beyond imagination, his mind is completely warped with the evil he projects, and he is the leader of the evil side. He devises the most horrible booby traps in the world-wide subway system. He longs to do something that will destroy the good guys because he believes that that there is more money to make by destruction of the world as we know it, than by preserving it for the future.

He has blonde hair and blue eyes, very slim built with a bone-chilling way of looking at a person that is very disconcerting. He has very advanced computer skills, and he likes to control people's lives with his hacking programs and other nonsense. His communication level is very high, and he thinks himself above the rest of the world. He worries about things needlessly, and he is known to cry when extremely frustrated. He experiments recklessly with drugs of many types and becomes very frightening at those times. He wants to destroy all that is good and wreak as much havoc on other people's lives as possible. Fashion is not something that is important to him. We will name him Alex. Alex prefers to be nondescript in dress and therefore wears the city colours of black, grey and beige. Dress him as you see fit.

The next avatar is a tall, red head, super girl, wearing grey tights and a rust jacket. She possesses a super nerdy type of face with glasses. She is one of the good guys, a researcher beyond compare. She finds out all the information about the world-wide system and gets the layout of the Smithsonian. Which is kept top-secret, yet she somehow manages to find out. She researches all the different angles that you make up for the game. So, go to it and make it as imaginative as possible. Wearing her white lab coat over her tights and turtleneck, her name is Negrecia and she is the ultimate good gal.

DRAW THIS AVATAR

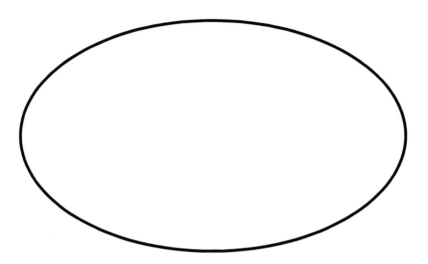

The next avatar is a white blonde girl, with a pixie haircut and emerald green eyes. Her hair spiky and she is truly evil. She helps with the plotting of the downfall of the good guys. She wears Doc Martens and cropped wide leg plants. She has an athletic build with a large bust line. Her voice is very sing song and she carries herself in a very athletic way. She has a way about her that holds people close while stabbing them in the back at the same time. She is tough and resourceful but commands very little respect with her peers. Tall, tough, blonde with attitude! She has a gift for numbers which helps her calculate distances, electric charges, and she understands the potential power in the blue diamond. Her family owns the company that the citizens of the world must pay to get their licenses from for fresh air and water. They are billionaires, therefore she never wants the world to be clean for everyone, only for the ones who can afford to pay. Her name is Anet and you should dress her anyway you want. Remember that her soul is evil and dark.

DRAW ANET

The next avatar is a girl, with black wavy hair, a small face and tiny, even, white teeth. She is short and petite, likes to wear a red shirt, a big trendy necklace, (a different one every day), black knee-high boots.

Hailey is a musician and a singer with an amazing imagination, her imagination is what helped her to solve the different challenges that were thrown in the way of the group. She can put herself into the mind of the evil one's without taking on their characteristics. She is an excellent problem solver. One of the good guys!

Sarah is tall and slim. She can fly like Maxine, in fact she is Maxine's cousin. Sarah likes to work with mechanical things and would fix everyone's Ebike for them. She wears black turtle necks and has short dark curly hair. Big green eyes and a spontaneous laugh, a joyful disposition yet thought as well. She is very kind and a dancer, boy can she dance. Her whole face lights up hen she dances. Something she does at the craziest times with great joy. She keeps the group going mechanically and physiologically. The good team!

Then there is tiny Michele, she has a cute physical presence with a magic twinkle in her brown eyes

She giggles with a charming abundance. The people in both the groups come to her for guidance but she is a member of the good side. She has a sharp wit and knows that sometimes things aren't always what they seem. It is her job to help the bad guys who have an obligation to do better so that the world can have clean air and water again, so that global warming and its effects will stop. She spends a lot of her time and energy with the third avatar to help him develop the conscious he needs to make him a better person make him a better person so that he can unlock the key.

She wears dresses with little shoes, even on her e-bike. She has a daughter who is a member of the good side as well, her daughter is very young, and Michelle protects her fiercely from the dark people.

DRAW THE DAUGHTER

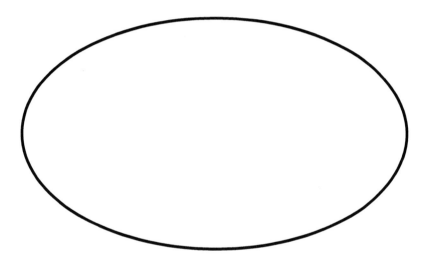

On the dark side there is one more man. His name is Audrey, he recruits all the little soldiers into the dark side, he sells them on the points of being on the evil side of things. He believes he is doing the right thing, he is another one of Michelle's challenges. He teaches all the kids on the dark side to ride through the tunnels and how to escape all the challenges the good side sends their way. He is very good at making sure they know how to meet every challenge.

Now make sure you make the challenges interesting and multi-levelled.

All the avatars in the game ride e-bikes through the worldwide subway system, the bad guys ride the Rudger. A big, black bike with a solid fit on the road. It has fat tires and a big black seat which could seat two if necessary in a race. The two headlights at the front of the bike have cages over them and the handle bars sit high on the front on the bike. It is all black and has a sinister look to it.

The good guys all ride the Diam, a low to the ground bike that almost resembles a big scooter but with a lot more power. It has beautiful lines and rides quietly through the city streets. There is one big headlight at the front. And it has a visible piston on the side.

Home at Last (Until the Next Adventure)

Physically something had started to happen to me, do you see it? My legs and arms reappeared during my deep thought process of the game. I had spun a silk cocoon around myself. I created my own think tank, now that the thought pattern was complete. I had metamorphosed, that word I couldn't think of in science class. The cocoon was completely gone, and I had become a beautiful butterfly. My wings they were a majestic purple, with tiny sparkles and then suddenly an idea came in my head and I started to move them in the motion of flying and yep fell right on my face. The livelihood and the joy disappeared, but then I closed my eyes and wished deep inside that my timing was right to go home. The next part of my adventure was to go home, to restart my life where I left off and to move forward.

I perceived this notion that I would be able to fly when I had become the person I was supposed to be. Where my head and my heart would be aligned within the right place.

Ok so let's see where is the right place? Can you tell me where it is?

Going back to the man and our work together I decided that I had to go find my way home, and I thanked him and went on my way, but I knew that we would meet again in another time in a different way. My heart told me that it would not be the last time that I saw him and as I walked I turned around many times to watch him and he never moved just watched me walk until I couldn't see him anymore and I felt strangely empty.

As I walked down the road I had a funny sensation of being watched, I kept turning around and looking but seeing nothing. Not nice, but somehow comforting someone was watching over me. Hmmm I wonder who that could be. I fell asleep under a big tree and when I woke up I stood up and began to fly to really fly and I knew then somewhere in all this time my heart and my head had aligned, I had metamorphosed fulfilling my foreshadowing thought in science class.

At last I was in my home town and I flew right over to my home and walked in the door, I became the same person physically as I was when I left. I looked around the house and everything was different. There was a science project on the table, and a tennis racket at the door with my name on it, I wondered if I was any good? (small slip back into the old me, it will still happen occasionally but only once in awhile).

I saw my dad and wondered what he was going to say he looked up and said, "Hi my girl, how was your sleep?" I smiled as I came to the realization that I hadn't missed anytime here I had just come back changed and somehow that change had changed everything around me.

At school that morning everything was so happy and calm, I found my mind alive with questions and answers about my studies some of the things I had talked about with the man I worked with all those months helped me and I realized how intelligent he truly was. I still had the feeling of being watched, strange but comforting, ok so as we end our story how do you see this ending?

In my own ending the feeling of comfort was the feeling of growth and wholeness I felt with the man who I worked beside for so many months.

We stayed together forever, and he became my life partner and we taught our butterflies to sleep together wrapped in each other's arms and be each other's partners in every way, always and forever. Because I am a girl, I will never tell anyone the end of my story just in case I jinx it. Also, because it comes after the other adventures of Harmony; even though he becomes part of the story as you will see.

This is the story of Harmony and the change of her life's ways. Try to remember to think of positive, good things when you try to find the right way every day. Hard work, but we must all do it.

DRAW YOUR OWN HARMONY

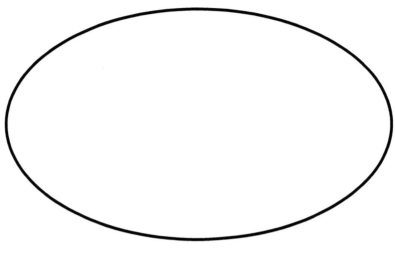

The Goal

Thank you so much for reading and participating in the book Harmony. The goal is to start a train of thought that will help you become the person you want to be not the person that other people want you to be.

A Series of Questions

Next there are a series of questions which you can choose to answer or not, where you can write down your thoughts on what you read in Harmony and about some other subjects that are on the top of the pages of the book as well as the blank pages. I hope that you will take your book with you everywhere and write in it with pleasure.

Ok, the first thought of all of this at the page you should write down five things that really made you smile today. Like the look on our mom's face when you tell her you love her and want to be just like her when you grow up.

Think of the qualities you want to possess and if you possess them now or not?

_____

_____

_____

_____

_____

The ABC's of Life

The ABC's of Life – take the words and add more of your own or pictures of other words that appeal to you. Use your imagination and remember there are no wrong answers in this part of the book or any other part of the book.

A- Adventure   B- Belief

C – Comfort

D – Dignity

SENSE WORTHINESS HONESTY
PRINCIPLES RESPONSIBILITY VALUES RESPECTABILITY TREATMENT
FAITH INTEGRITY SOCIAL
MOTIVATION THEORY EQUALITY TRUTH
HYPOCRISY ETHICS CONVENTIONALITIES
PHILISOPHY MORALS AUTHENTICITY
PERFORMANCE TRUST RULES INNOCENCE CHARACTER
ETIQUETTE HONOR
FAIRNESS CRITERIA DECENCY VIRTUE PURPOSE INNOCENCE FAIRNESS
RESPECT STANDARDS ATTITUDE ACCEPTANCE CONDUCT

_____

_____

_____

_____

_____

_____

_____

_____

E – Elephants

F-Feelings

_____

_____

_____

_____

_____

_____

_____

_____

G – Grace

H – Harmony

_____
_____
_____
_____
_____
_____
_____
_____
_____

I – Intelligence

J – Joyful

_____
_____
_____
_____
_____
_____
_____
_____

K – Kool-Aid

L – Love

_____
_____
_____
_____
_____
_____
_____
_____

M – Music

N – Nice

_____

_____

_____

_____

_____

_____

_____

_____

O – Opportunities

P – People

_____

_____

_____

_____

_____

_____

_____

_____

_____

Q – Question

R – Rose

S – Swan

T – Time

_____

_____

_____

_____

_____

_____

_____

_____

U – Unique

V – Valentines

W – Wind

X – Xylophone

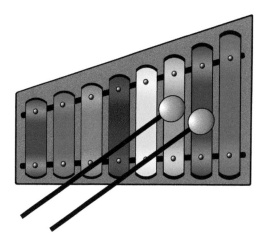

Y – Yoga

Z – Zebra

CPSIA information can be obtained
at www.ICGtesting.com
Printed in the USA
BVHW021132071118
532428BV00025B/1197/P

9 781982 208714